WALMINGT[...]
CARNIVO[...]
MASTER BUTCHER!

JACK JONES THE BUTCHER

KU-534-106

FOR WHEN YOU WANT BOTH BRAINS AND BRAWN!

Ever since being a young lad in the Boer War I've known how to wield the cold steel so why not come and try my fresh cuts? Famed throughout the south coast, well, maybe not the entire south coast, as that's a lot isn't it? Certainly this side of Eastbourne. Though not as far as Brighton, no... There's a chap in Brighton that makes faggots that just melt in the mouth, beautiful they are... he's probably the most well-known butcher in that neck of the woods. I'm famed within the general area anyway. Well, maybe "famed" isn't the word either really, I mean it's not as if I'm Clark Gable is it? Not that the ladies don't love a butcher! All you need's a piece of kidney and a cheeky wink! What was I saying... Must be careful, the chap at the printer said I could only have 200 words before I run out of... Oh... sausages...

THE WALMINGTON-ON-SEA
HOME GUARD
TRAINING MANUAL

THE WALMINGTON-ON-SEA
HOME GUARD
TRAINING MANUAL

CAPTAIN GEORGE MAINWARING
AND MEMBERS OF HIS PLATOON

I really do think I should get a credit here, sir.
After all, I've spent all this time going through
the book and making sure we all come out looking
rather marvellous. Something simple like "Edited by
Sergeant Arthur Wilson" will do.

CONTENTS

INTRODUCTION
BY CAPTAIN GEORGE MAINWARING

SOME people are born for danger. It occurred to me the other day, while watching the fine fighting men of my platoon get their breath back after map-reading practice, that I am one of those people. When all seems lost I am at my very best. Why, only the other day when I was informed that we were low on change behind the counter of Swallow's Bank [Walmington-on-Sea branch] I did not panic, nor lose my head. No. I simply had our chief clerk call around a few of our regular business customers in order to replenish supply. A weaker man would have crumbled.

This daredevil streak is not without direction. Quite the contrary. I offer it, with the proud sanction of the pips on my shoulder, to the defence of my country. ←

whether it wants it or not!

As captain, I have lead our local Home Guard force to *(1)* victory time and again. Nothing could make me prouder. Those pips mean the world, a sign of respect offered by the whole town. A thanks for a job well done. Of course, *(2)* it was only natural that I should be selected for command given my experience and rank during the last war. Back then there was no holding me back either, the moment we declared war on Germany I rushed to enlist. It's true that my eyesight was deemed a problem for the rather narrow-minded enrolment board but I didn't give up and soon took up my post in France. *(3)*

1. Well really sir, 'leading to victory'? That seems somewhat excessive given our lack of actual combat.
2. Actually sir, if you recall you conferred the rank on yourself. Perhaps I should edit for clarity?
3. Five years later, after hostilities had ended. Do you want me to clarify that point sir?

You can imagine my determination to return to the fighting ranks when Germany once more made its presence felt on the global stage. When Mr. Eden called for the formation of the Local Defence Volunteers I was at the very front of the queue and inspiring my *(4)* subordinates at the bank to do the same. A man simply cannot stand by and let others dictate his fate. We must listen to our inner voice and not follow blindly in the paths of others. If there's one thing I hope I've instilled in my men it's that instinct to be your own man. That and an unswerving need to obey orders.

Since that defining moment when I stood up to *(5)* occupy my rank, I have given my life in the defence of this country, dedicating every spare minute to the preparation and training of my unit against the inevitable invasion. Night after night we gather in our makeshift barracks [the church hall, a hive of civil unrest I like to hope we have helped quash by our inspiring presence], rebuilding ourselves as fighting men for the modern age. My platoon has risen honourably to the challenge: Jack Jones our *(6)* local butcher, is once more the keen blade he proved to be in the last war; Joe Walker, a local trader of some ill-repute has shown the moral fibre hidden deep within, wearing his uniform with honour [a uniform that he helped keep in trim I must say, where would we have been *(7)* without his frequent provision of elastic and replacement buttons?]; Even young Pike, a boy almost crippled by his

I said I was sorry about that, my braces snapped!

mother's kindness has begun to show a good deal of pluck.

I believe he has even stopped crying during the blackouts.

Much to be proud of. Though the price has been not a moment's rest — my mind focused on the intricacies of military strategy during every waking hour, seven days a week. Yes! Even at the weekends my duty stands fast. Sundays are intended to be a quiet day, a day spent in happy relaxation with one's family and spouse. A day

---

4. I think forcing is the word you re after here sir.
5. Not literally, of course sir, otherwise you would be dead. Something I feel sure the platoon would have noticed.
6. Yes sir, very keen.
7. Wealthier, certainly, at his prices it would be cheaper to sew shillings on our jackets.

of jollity and laughter. I find that's rarely the case with my Elizabeth. In fact I am often forced to forego such pleasantries for a day of weapon-stripping and emergency work within the Anderson shelter. She wouldn't have it any other way, she's a tartar when it comes to duty. Or anything else come to that.

Some men would not be able to take such pressure, they would break beneath the constant responsibility. Not me. If anything, I find the experience sharpens my abilities, every ounce of my military training honed keenly against the whetstone of the Nazi Horror.

So, let them come! They will not find the good men and women of Walmington-on-Sea napping.

What if its night-time? I cant stay awake too late; mum would kill me.

Given that the Home Guard has been my life, it was only a matter of time before I was asked to set my thoughts down on paper. So, why await the inevitable? A good officer knows to anticipate orders. Some might criticise my 'jumping the gun' in this regard but there's no time for that sort of thing; this book could save lives.

Within these pages myself and those loyal men under me will seek to pass on the considerable wisdom of our years. We are not saying that our way is the only way but let me ask you this: how safe do the citizens of Walmington-on-Sea feel when they tuck themselves up for the night? Precisely. Our warm presence can be felt in the bedrooms of the whole town. And they say we're past our prime!

I have divided the text into three sections: firstly initial preparation, then the various skills needed in the field. Finally, combat itself. In-between these sections myself and select members of my platoon will pose revision questions designed to ensure that you have remembered all you have read. This book is everything you need to turn a platoon of men into a platoon of soldiers, it will guide you towards a safer, better Home Guard. And with that we can look to a safer, better Britain!

Is that what Uncle Arthur's doing here at night? Making mum and I feel safe?

Thanks Uncle Arthur!

Captain G Mainwaring

EDITOR'S NOTE
BY SERGEANT ARTHUR WILSON

What a frightful photograph
of me. Can we get a better
one, sir?

Wilson.

I HAVE been asked by Captain Mainwaring to add a short note expressing my feelings over the last few years, working alongside the platoon and training in the many and diverse arts of war. "Write something inspiring," he asks, "summing up how the experience has changed your life for the better."

Well, as you know, it can be dreadfully difficult to think of the words when one is put on the spot but I shall do my best:

It's all been rather lovely.

Except for those occasions when it wasn't.

The Honourable Arthur Wilson Esq.

SECTION ONE
BE PREPARED

GIVEN the rigours of <u>modern combat</u> it is vitally *(1)* important that today's soldier is fully prepared. It is every commanding officer's duty to spend the weeks needed bringing his men up to fighting standard. It is not just a matter of training but also disposition. It *(2)* takes a <u>very special sort of man</u> to fill his uniform, wield his backpack and be prepared to kill with his bare hands if necessary.

Over the next few pages myself and the men of the Walmington-on-Sea platoon will cover the basic preparations to be considered before setting foot in the field.

Always wear your wellies, that's what mum says, dirty places fields.

1. As opposed to the carefree warfare of old?
2. Or perhaps just a varied selection of average ones?

PART I - UNIFORM
BY CAPTAIN GEORGE MAINWARING

"Clothes make the man," as Shakespeare once said. *(1)*
Has that ever been more the case than with a soldier?
There's not many who can be unaware they're in the
presence of a military man when he's in uniform.

Unless they were blind and the soldier very very quiet.

You just can't beat the impression created by finely-
pressed fatigues. The crispness of each crease, the gleam
(2) of the buttons, the stiff, unassailable collar. Everything
a soldier can say about his country is right there in the
uniform. *Tight in the lower regions and smelly when wet!*

Let's take a look at how to create the best impression
shall we?

CAP: Perfectly placed, just a few degrees off north. You can
tell a lot about a man by the angle of his hat, the further
to one side he wears it the looser are his scruples. If you
have the misfortune of spending any time with a man in a
lopsided Trilby then for goodness sake check your wallet
afterwards.

1. It was Mark Twain actually sir. Very witty man,
extremely quotable. 'All you need is ignorance and
confidence, then success is sure.' That was one of
his too.
2. And if you give the cuffs one roll back from the
wrist it sets the whole off a treat.

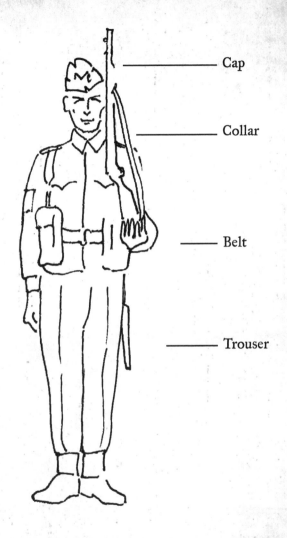

Cap

Collar

Belt

Trouser

Fig 1.1.1: A sharp soldier.

COLLAR: These should be pressed so as to form a perfect defensive wall around the neck. Nothing about a man should be allowed to flop about, certainly not his collar.

BELT: Perfectly cinched so as to neither crumple the uniform nor allow it to fall off [though a wise man will have his braces on too, this country didn't get where it was by putting all its eggs in one basket].

TROUSER: There's a reason all gents wear a crease in their trouser, not only does it improve the hang of the garment but it has also been <u>proven by our military scientists</u> to cut [3] down on wind-resistance and thereby improve marching speed.

BOOTS: I know there's a worrying habit in modern soldiering to apply excess amounts of dubbin to the boots in order to make them supple and thereby more comfortable. They say the waterproofing qualities of the wax is also extremely beneficial. Well, I don't know about that, but I do know that anyone who wants a respectable shine on their leather reaches for the polish and ignores such namby-pamby concerns. What's more important? Comfort and durability in the damp or a gleaming pair of boots? Precisely. The day we shirk from blisters and water in this country is the day we deserve invasion.

---

3. I suspect this to be what is known in espionage circles as a "lie".

Now let's look at the alternative shall we? The sort of shabby ne'er-do-well that often turns up on the first day of enrolment. We shouldn't treat him too roughly, with some gentle guidance and a righteous kick up the backside he may one day make a proper soldier.

Hitler has very neat hair too, mum says its one of the few good things about him.

Fig 1.1.2: A shambles of a soldier.

HAIR: Have they never heard of Brylcreem? As tousled and greasy as a startled goat. No man ever became great with wild looking hair. Look at Churchill or Baldwin, men who knew to keep hair to a well-oiled minimum.

UNSHAVEN: I blame the cinema. It seems that some men today equate an unshaven chin with masculinity. Well, it may look good on a cowboy but it doesn't pass muster in our fine forces. Randolph Scott? Raymond Hatton? No thanks, bunch of pansies with questionable politics, give me a real hero like Lord Baden-Powell.

CIGARETTE: Puffing away like a steamship, not on my watch! If you must smoke cigarettes then restrict their consumption to an appropriate time. *(4)*

BUTTONS: How lazy must a man be not to replace a button? All it takes is some strong thread and a few minutes of your wife's time.

CREASED UNIFORM: Not only does it look untidy but you may be mistaken for one of the more crumpled nations. What's worse? A few minutes pressing your uniform or a bullet in the back when taken for an Italian spy?

PUTTEES: It's not complex geometry, they should be worn at an even height, an absolute fool could do it. *Thats not true, mine always end up sagging after a good march*

An out and out shambles from top to bottom. A true soldier should be respectable in appearance. "Would you invite him home to tea?" I often ask, when faced with a dogs dinner of military dress. Certainly, nothing less than the perfect fighting man would be safe if presented to my Elizabeth.

Of course with cutbacks affecting many Home Guard platoons you may not be lucky enough to be issued with the correct uniform. You'll find no man more disappointed than me with the meagre budget offered to the Home Guard but one must rise to the challenge and show a little initiative. Make a lot of the little you have, it's the British way.

So, let's look at how a perfectly respectable combat uniform can be fashioned from everyday items available to any Home Guard recruit:

HELMET: When the bombs are falling only a fool goes out unprotected. I recommend a solid pudding basin [or bread bin for those with above-average hat-size]. Thanks to extensive testing by our very own Lance Corporal Jones and members of the local cricket team I can attest that, with the addition of chin strap and padding, a soldier can take a number of solid blows to the skull before passing out.

4. I often find one most relaxing after training. it has quite the calming effect. Actually during can often be necessary too.

TIE AND COLLAR: There's no need for a slovenly neckline, besides, a tie can double up as bandage or even garrotte in the field. Never be afraid to think of your wardrobe in terms of practicality as well as appearance. Could your braces double up as a catapult? Your belt as a whip?

You could wave your shirt when you need to surrender!

In the right hands almost anything can become formidable. A regular exercise in our platoon involves my selecting a common household object and asking the platoon how it could be adapted into a weapon. Only the other week we had countless suggestions of how to cripple a man using nothing more than a pair of a nutcrackers.

SUIT: You may not have tunic and trousers but that's no excuse to let appearances slide. A suit commands confidence and respect. Do you really think we would have had once owned half the world were it not for our immaculate appearance? The enemy cannot fail but know you mean business when you come looming out of the gloom at them in a well-cut suit.

PACK: You'll still need to carry your supplies so make sure you kit yourself out with a satchel or other, easily portable carrier. It's a slack soldier that relies on his pockets, imagine the delay caused by a man ferreting past corned-beef sandwiches and tobacco tins in order to reach his air-raid whistle. Satchels save lives!

Fig 1.1.3: A suited man, soldiering on.

PART 2 - EQUIPMENT
BY PRIVATE JOE WALKER

This image will need to be centred on the page.

WHEN fighting a war people think the only equipment you need is a gun. Nothing could be further from the truth. For months down here in Walmington the closest we got to a rifle was reading Boy's Own over Pikey's shoulder. The only weapons we had were a rusty bayonet and Frazer's breath. If Hitler had invaded in the early days of the Home Guard we'd have been fighting him off with catapults and conkers.

Weapons aren't everything. A soldier needs a lot of equipment in order to defend Home and Country.

Nothing's more important than having the right kit; if there's one thing missing it could mean the difference between life and death. A girl I knew used to say: 'What's the use having a rifle if you ain't got the ammo!' Wise words. Not that she was what you'd call an ideal "target"! It certainly wouldn't take much of an aim; you'd find shapelier ankles on the Michelin Man. Seriously, I could have earned a living hiring her underwear out as circus venues, could have done with the money and all... you needed a bank loan to take her out for dinner, never saw a dessert trolley she didn't take for a spin.

Anyway, I'm wandering off the point. *(1)*

I've been asked to run through some basic supplies for the Home Guard soldier who wants to keep ahead, concentrating on the homemade additions a fella can gather himself. After all, no use relying on the equipment they dole out is there? A broom handle and a can-opener? What's a soldier to do with that, open a can of peas at a safe distance? Nah... if you want half a chance of making it through an invasion with your particulars still in place you just pay attention to your Uncle Joe.

I. He is rather. It may be jolly but I can hear
   Mainwaring now "If I'd wanted Arthur Askey to
   write the section I'd have asked him"

DAYTIME:

1. *NEWSPAPER* — Can't go wrong with a copy of The Mirror can you? Something to take your mind off things when its dry and a perfectly serviceable rain hat when it's not.

2. *NOTEBOOK AND PEN* — Always make sure you can take notes when you're out and about. How else do you keep track of all the orders, bets and phone numbers? Oh, and soldiery stuff like... erm.. co-ordinates, secret codes, you know, that sort of thing.

3. *GROUNDSHEET/CAPE* — If you're lucky enough to be one of the handful of units in the country to have been issued with your full kit then you'll have your waterproofs. If not find your closest incontinent duffer

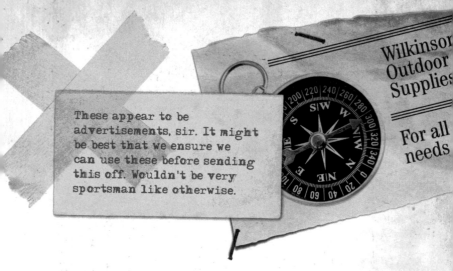

Wilkinson
Outdoor
Supplies

For all
needs

These appear to be advertisements, sir. It might be best that we ensure we can use these before sending this off. Wouldn't be very sportsman like otherwise.

[likely the bloke stood next to you on parade] and see if he'll let you have a rubber bed sheet. A bit of trimming and these do a perfect job. Also perfect for picnics and those moments when you and a friend may want to spread out on the grass for a bit. Do wash it first though, if ladies liked the smell of old latrines they'd have bottled it.

4. *COMPASS* — Joe's Quick Guide to Using a Compass: Get it out, wave it around a bit, just so that everyone sees you and knows you're the sort of bloke that can do clever things like read a compass. Then put it away and ask someone for directions. Why make a meal out of things? You're the Home Guard! If you can't find your way around your own manor without a bloomin' compass there's no hope for you.

BRITISH MADE

BRYMAY

SAFETY MATCHES

NIGHTTIME:

1. *TORCH* — Yeah, yeah, 'put that light out'... Still, if you're in the middle of nowhere you'll definitely need one. It's no fun nipping off into the bushes for a jimmy riddle when it's black as pitch [just ask Private Godfrey to tell you about the gentleman's boots he mistook for a tree root, Godfrey got his first experience of enemy insertion that night, I can tell you!].

2. *MATCHES* — Those snouts won't light themselves now will they?.

3. *SPADE* — If you're stuck out there you may as well do something to keep yourself warm, hadn't you? Last night I came home with ten spuds, three turnips and a few carrots. Dig for Victory? I'll say... Get yourself a

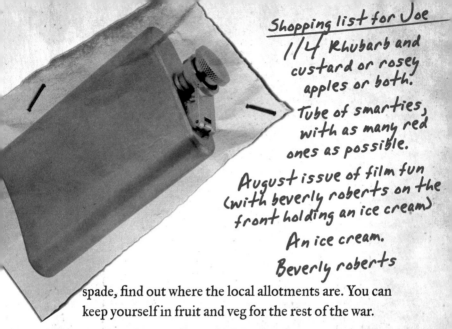

Shopping list for Joe

1/4 Rhubarb and custard or rosey apples or both.

Tube of smarties, with as many red ones as possible.

August issue of film fun (with beverly roberts on the front holding an ice cream)

An ice cream.

Beverly roberts

spade, find out where the local allotments are. You can keep yourself in fruit and veg for the rest of the war.

4. *WATERPROOF MAP POUCH* — Don't want your copy of Film Fun getting wet do you? Otherwise you'll have nothing to read while you wait for dawn.

5. *HIP FLASK* — No need to freeze to death is there? Think of it less as booze more as Naughty Horlicks.

Not that any of this is easy to come by of course. You can't get military supplies anywhere these days. After all, there is a war on. Though, come to think of it, I might be able to do you a favour... Just phone the Church Hall, Walmington-on-Sea 333, and ask for Private Walker. Patriotic prices guaranteed...

PART 3 - WEAPONRY
BY LANCE-CORPORAL JACK JONES

Sir,
I've got these
few photographs
of me, ready for
printing sir.
Sorry some of
them are a bit
battered, sir,
on account of
the shoe box the
were kept in
being slightly
roughed up by
small lavatory
plumbing upset, sir.

Permission to write sir! *(1)*

It is a great honour to be asked by my commanding officer Mr. Mainwaring to add to this wonderful book what will be written by him in what I am sure will be a very *(2)* illustrated manner showing the aims and also the pitbulls of modern warfare which is a subject very close to our hearts having both served in the previous war and that will inspire all readers and then be printed by my friend Bob at his work which is a printers and very good at it he is too.

I would like to discuss the subject of weaponry. Weaponry is to the experienced soldier what a skin is to a sausage: without it you'd be knee deep in guts! Just my little joke there, got to smile haven't you? Not that you would smile if you were knee deep in guts mind you. No. I imagine smiling would be the last thing on your mind in that situation. You would probably be more inclined to do a lot of shouting. Or, in the worst case, a lot of dying. During my time in the Sudan I saw a great deal of both and, for sure, I would have joined in where it not for my trusty bayonet. Which goes to prove the point I believe I was originally making. Weapons are very useful things indeed.

1. Permission granted.
2. I feel we may want to give this sentence a bit of a once over.

I remember one night in particular. Our camp was ambushed by the Dervishes, they'd killed the sentries and we'd have all gone the same way... they were devilish swine the Dervishes you know, open you up like a suitcase so they would, a suitcase full of offal... not that you'd ever carry offal in a suitcase of course, it would stain the leather, and likely drip everywhere, ruin the carpet... I don't imagine they'd let you travel with one either, not through Customs, offal must be the sort of thing that Customers frown on I'd have thought. Doesn't matter how spot on your passport was, a bag full of kidneys would not be allowed across the border. You get my meaning though, about the Dervishes, vicious, have your gizzards in their teeth as soon as look at you.

(3)   So, the Dervishes were advancing on our tents and would have done for the lot of us were it not for the fact that I was wide-awake due to a spot of the old belly trouble. I'd taken some bicarb [Kitchener once said to me. 'A soldier marches on bicarb' which isn't altogether true, he marches on his feet but I think what he meant to say was we'd be lost without it, well not lost because we had maps didn't we? But we'd be in some distress... certainly I was often very glad of it and still am now, always keep your bicarb close to hand, that's the point isn't it? I think.]. So, I'd had some bicarb and was passing the time while waiting for it to work by

3. I have a terrible fear we may have to get someone else to write this section. I know it's a subject dear to his heart but there's a very real chance that the war will be over before he makes his point.

cleaning my bayonet, getting a good gleam on it, keeping that blade sharp. You never know when you'll need it. In fact I was just about to need it, so that was quite lucky.

So, the Dervishes were advancing and we wouldn't have known a thing because they had a devilish skill for silence like nobody else I've ever seen. You'll never hear a Dervish sneaking up on you. No. Imagine a mouse wrapped in cotton wool and wearing carpet slippers, that's what the Dervishes were like. Not to look at obviously, they were considerably larger than mice and wouldn't have dreamed of wearing carpet slippers in the desert. Too hot. You'd get foot rot. I couldn't say for sure whether they had access to cotton wool either but I suspect not. Can't see they would have a use for it. Certainly they were quiet enough without it. Devilishly quiet they were, you'd never hear one creep up on you.

I certainly didn't and would have paid for it with my life were it not for the fact that, troubled by a particularly strong bout of stomach cramps, I had bent over just as one of the Dervishes leapt on me from behind. In that position I would have certainly been savagely seen to, were it not for the fact that I still had a firm grip on my weapon. My arms crossed, the blade was sticking out behind me — much to the Dervish's loud distress when he jumped onto it. Hence the saying: 'Look before you leap.'

So, let's look at bladed weapons in detail:

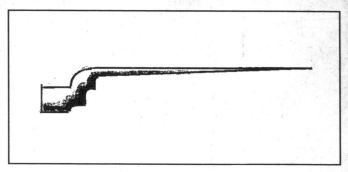

Fig 1.3.1: They do not like it up 'em

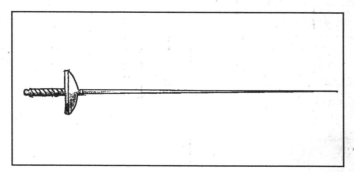

Fig 1.3.2: They do not like it up 'em

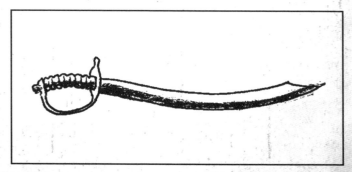

Fig 1.3.3: They do not like it up 'em

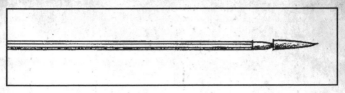

Fig 1.3.4: They do not like it up 'em

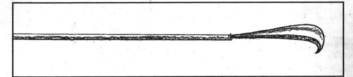

Fig 1.3.5: They do not like it up 'em

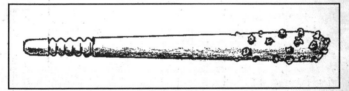

Fig 1.3.6: They do not like it up 'em

The hole made by the bayonet [Fig 1.3.1] can easily be confused with the hole made by the 303 bullet what is a similar size. The dervishes will not be confused because they will probably be dead. These holes can sometimes be oval shaped like a hard boiled egg what has been sat on. This is because the dervishes are often whirling dervishes who keep on whirling and whirling round and round to avoid having it up them which they do not like but the result is an oval shaped hole. Properly trained British soldiers know this well.

I can't say that I'm fond
of this one either, sir.
I appear to be scowling.
I don't scowl.
Wilson.

NOTHING unites a group of able-bodied, highly trained, fighting men more than drill practice. It teaches discipline, creates a sharp ear for orders and... well, it just looks dreadfully impressive. It really does; all those neat rows, the thump of leather on concrete; it's terribly, terribly good.

So how does one achieve such precision and uniformity? An excellent question and one that I have often wished someone would answer. Still, there's no point in letting these little things get in the way, one can only build walls using the bricks one has to hand.

Accepting then that there's no such thing as perfection, let's look at how to get the best one can out of the men.

VOICE: A lot of successful drill training is down to the voice of command. I know it's frightfully common to have the Drill Sergeant barking his orders out with all the affability of a bull in an air-raid but I've never found the need. One just likes to show a touch of civility, appealing to the men's sense of fair play and ask if they might sort of 'fall-in' and then take it from there.

Many Drill Sergeant's swear by what they call "DLIPS" a frightfully clever acronym for Distinctness, Loudness, Inflection, Precision and Snap.

or "Don't Laugh if Pike Slips-Up"!

Some Underwear Pinches Everyones Rear!

Personally I stand by my own method: Soldiers/ Understand Perfect English Readily or "SUPER". There really is no need to start treating them like a pack of naughty labradors. Just tell them what you'd like them to do and they'll probably do it.

Once they're in position and ready for the off, there are lots of things we can ask them to do... it's all rather like 'Simon Says' but slightly more limited, one really can't ask them to start jumping up and down or tapping their heads while rubbing their stomachs, while awfully clever these things are distinctly frowned upon on parade [1] grounds I understand. Never mind, let's look at the basic moves shall we?

First of all we have a couple of different types of standing.

ATTENTION: When one asks the ranks [that is to say: rows] to kindly stand to attention, they straighten up, legs together, arms by their side all rather like chaps that have been caught in the act, ramrod straight and ready for a dressing down from sir. It does look frightfully good but one can't expect them to stand like that forever — most especially our platoon. If they're tense for more than half a minute you can hear the 'twang' of medical supports

1. And frightfully difficult to do without chuckling, something else they don't like to see during parade.

The edges will need trimming off of this one, sir

snapping. It's like a string quartet under attack. To avoid this, we would definitely employ the "at ease" position [see below]. Before we get to that though there is a lovely little "extra" to the "attention" position which can look jolly impressive if played right. That is:

PRESENT ARMS: Now, by arms what we actually mean is rifles not the soldiers' arms, that wouldn't look good at all. When we shout "present arms" then those carrying a rifle would hold it vertically and to their side, as if ready to go into battle. Those without rifles would salute. It's all very showy. So, once we've had a nice go at that then we return to the "attention" position briefly before letting everyone relax and adopting the other type of standing we like in the army:

AT EASE: Don't let the name fool you! It's not really at ease, say leaning against a warm fire sipping a brandy and smoking a cigarette, they don't go in for that much in the army. It's 'at ease' in comparison to the standing to attention [but then, frankly, what isn't?]. The soldiers part their legs a little, arms clasped behind the back. Rather like you were waiting for a bus.

When 'at ease' you can tell them any outstanding business, explain plans, give notices and what have you. If they manage to stay awake through that, it's time for the marching.

MARCHING: Now, all marching leads from the left foot

unless expressly ordered otherwise. I have no idea why. Bearing that in mind — and you will have the most terrible mess if you don't — the drill sergeant suggests that the chaps might like to "about turn" which should have them all whisking around at a ninety degree angle anti-clockwise [you would say "by the right" if you wanted them to go the other way I suppose, though I rarely think of that as it would see us all marching into the vicar's office and that never ends well. Vicar's offices are simply far too small and clerical to parade in, the stationery always gets damaged as do the men]. Then you would suggest they march — or "quick march" or "on the double" it all rather depends if you're in a hurry or not. In my experience you usually are, an army moves at two speeds: "quickly now!" or "oops too late!" — and off they go, swinging the left leg first and then the right. Once all the chaps get this it should look quite splendid as they trot off in unison.

You're bound to have the odd fellow who loses rhythm, I mean, some of us have it and some of us just don't. Same
(1) with dancing isn't it? There will always be chaps with two left feet. Just try to jolly them along and if all else fails shove them in the middle where they don't make such a beastly eyesore of themselves.

I. I've always had a devil of a foxtrot and can cross a dance floor in the blink of an eye. It's all in the music though, isn't it? I did ask Captain Mainwaring if we could pop a record on during parade but he wouldn't have it.

While marching there are several commands one can give:

EYES RIGHT: Or, for that matter, left I suppose... this command has everyone turning their heads sharply in the direction given so that they can offer their attention to a commanding officer or anything else you particularly want them to see [though don't make the mistake I did and suggest the gentlemen take in a particular view, the army is frightfully opposed to such things as nice views and the drill sergeant will often get a veritable earful should he go against the flow of this thinking].

RIGHT/LEFT TURN: Obviously there will come a time when it simply isn't practical for the parade to keep marching in a straight line. There are all sorts of hazards such as steps, rivers and brick walls which necessitate the application of a bit of steering. One simply suggests the requisite direction before the chaps end up falling over. I know it seems as if one could just leave all this to the common sense of the fellows in front but the army isn't awfully keen on common sense — presumably noting a distinct lack of it amongst its troops — and does try not to rely on it if at all possible.

MARK TIME: Rather good if one is unsure whether one wants one's parade to turn left or right, jolly useful while one is checking a map say or asking a local for directions. At this order, the company simply marches on the spot, keeping the same rhythm as before but holding fire with regards actually going anywhere.

HALT: Well now, you hardly need me to explain this one, though it's best mentioned if only so that the correct term is understood. Commanding officers do not have a great deal of patience with paraphrasing on the parade ground. "That'll do now," or "Stop that then" are not deemed acceptable suggestions to the parade however much conviction you may say them with.

It's also important to give them a little warning, otherwise you'll end up with a pile of broken soldiers as they crash into one another. I favour a particularly elongated "compaaaaany" before the "halt". There will still be a considerable amount of foot shuffling, and what looks like an irish jig as they try and remember which foot they should be on, but at least you'll avoid any broken limbs.

RETIRE: This command is employed not, of course, in the occupational sense [in our case it would be a suggestion offered far too late in the day as most of them have] but rather in the more generalised sense of withdrawing from one place to another. When one suggests the parade retires one is telling them to head back in from the parade ground and call it a night [though they are expected to do this in formation until they have cleared the ground] as opposed to:

DISMISSED: An order that usually comes as a great relief to us all.

SECTION TEST

UNIFORM - A selection of questions provided by Private Charles Godfrey, former Gentlemen's Outfitter at the Army & Navy Stores.

1. Should a gentleman's cap be worn perfectly erect or just a little to the side?

Not like this!

A — 1. Just a little bit to the side is best, I often find that if it won't stay in place then a ladies hair grip can be most useful.

[There are no more questions on uniform as Private Godfrey has asked to be excused.]

INGENUITY - A multiple-choice question supplied by Private James Frazer:

You're behind the wheel of a Leyland 3-ton truck driving along a badly kept road in the middle of the night. The storm is lashing at your windows and the lightning cutting up the sky as if the devil hisself was abroad and watching your every step. You're tired and your eyelids are drooping despite the terrible conditions, you should stop... maybe take a wee nap... but you carry on.

A few minutes later the road in front of you is lit up once more by a flash of lightning and you clearly see the silhouette of a man not a few feet away. He's stood in the middle of the road, a knife in one hand and, hanging from the other, something with hair, something red, dripping

Could the printer centre this photograph of Frazer?

in the rain, pooling at the man's feet like a crimson pond in Hell!

You slam on the brakes and your vehicle careers out of control in the wet mud. The truck rolls! You scream! This is it! You just know it! This is the moment you die!

All goes black... Then, slowly you come around, bleary eyed and with a splitting headache. You cannae tell if the dampness in your hair is rain getting in from the smashed windscreen or blood from a cut in your scalp. You touch your forehead gently with your fingers and they come away red, red with the stain of your own blood! And that reminds you of what you saw... out there... in the darkness... in the rain... that... terrible THING that the man was holding... and are those footsteps you can hear above the sound of the rain? Heavy boots drawing closer and closer as he raises his knife in the moonlight, wanting to make sure the blade is keen for the work he has in mind. Could it be...? Aye! It could! He's getting closer and closer... you can almost feel him as he draws alongside the driver's cab and begins... slowly... to crouch down beside you.

Do you...?

A. Scream, the lightning drowning out the noise as he reaches through and cuts your head clean off with a swipe of his infernal blade?

B. Beg for mercy, but know all along that it's a waste of your final breath as you're doomed, DOOMED to die on this terrible stormy night.

C. Reach for the starting handle that was the only way of getting that damned Leyland running and brain that nutty bampot with it before he does for ye.

A —
C, you wet-headed fool.

EQUIPMENT - Questions supplied by Private Joe Walker

1. Where is it possible to find a decent compass?

2. Do you know a good supplier of elastic bands?

3. Isn't scotch for your hip flask impossible to get hold of?

I wonder if Joe can get Ovaltine?

4. Do we really need everything you suggest in your equipment section, even the rubber bands?

— A —

1. Funny you should ask that, I do have a couple on hand, give me a bell and I'll put one to one side for you.

2. It just so happens I do, a very good supplier of mine has plenty and is willing to part with them for what is, considering the quality, a very reasonable price.

3. Well, it isn't cheap of course but nothing's impossible. You know my motto: "Ask and ye shall receive [with discounts for bulk]."

4. Of course you do, I don't want you to panic but you'll most likely be dead within the week unless you put your hand in your pocket and start buying. I wouldn't lead you wrong now would I?

SECTION TWO
IN THE FIELD

Of course, being comfortable within the secure walls of command is all well and good but it's when playing away that the platoon needs to stand proud. For myself I am rarely happier than when out in the open, with nothing between me and the earth *(1)* but my wits. What a test of a man! Here then is all you need to know about field craft and soldiering away from HQ.

I. And a tent, a bed roll and the general assistance of your sergeant and the rest of the platoon.

PART I - FIELD CRAFT
BY CAPTAIN GEORGE MAINWARING

First things first, a soldier needs his camp, a base of operations, a place to rest and plan. *(1)*

1. CHOOSING A LOCATION

There are many considerations a commanding officer must make when selecting where his men should camp. Here is my simple checklist:

A) IS THE AREA EASY TO DEFEND?

This really is of tantamount importance. Who knows what devilish forces may set upon you at any moment? You must ensure clear lines of sight at all times. It's no *(2)* good camping in a forest clearing, for example, who knows what could be using the shadows of the trees for cover?

B) DOES IT OFFER NATURAL AMENITIES?

Is there fresh water close to hand? A supply of wood for the fire? Is it sheltered from the wind or rain? *(3)* The great outdoors is filled with practical benefits for the canny camper, make the most of your environment!

C) CHECK YOUR EXIT

(4) Don't be caught napping! When Fritz comes at you, always have your escape route open. Not that I advocate

simply running away in the face of the danger, where would we be if the British Forces had that attitude? Huddled together in Greenland surrounded by the Nazi menace! But if the filthy swine start dropping bombs on you or advancing in tanks there's only one thing a sensible commanding officer can do: call for a strategic withdrawal. Rest assured it won't be long before Tommy Atkins is back on the offensive, you can't keep solid, British strategic thinking down for long, we invented it! (5)

D) IS THE GROUND SOFT ENOUGH TO DIG?

Of course, a gentleman doesn't like to make too much of it but latrines are needed for any camp. In fact, in the case of my platoon it's often the first task. The only complication being where they're supposed to relieve themselves while the digging is still in progress.

1. And itch. And freeze. And ache. Only cows and idiots feel joyous about loitering in fields.
2. At night? How is one supposed to achieve that one wonders?
3. Is there a decent hotel nearby?
4. Unless, of course, they happen to attack when you're asleep in which case you can hardly avoid it
5. Tell that to a Roman, I believe the "strategic" British response when they invaded was to hide in holes flinging mud at passing centurions.

2. PITCHING YOUR TENT

Awkward this... I had asked my Sergeant to prepare some words explaining, step by step, how the tent was put together. He has often been involved in this sort of thing during exercises and it seemed sensible to ask him to handle the relevant part of this chapter. Of course, needless to say, head in the clouds as always, he has failed to provide me with anything. It's most frustrating. I distinctly said to him, 'Wilson,' I said 'Write me a piece about the erecting of tents.' No matter, I shall just have to do it myself. The process is perfectly simple, after all, an idiot could do it.

A) FIRST, UNPACK YOUR CANVAS AND CONSTRUCTION POLES.

B) THEN PUT IT ALL TOGETHER...

3. CAMP FIRE

Every camp needs a fire of course, both for warmth and cooking upon. If morale is low one can also sing songs around them I believe, though it's not something I've encouraged myself. We did let Private Frazer tell a story once, something ludicrous involving a lighthouse and a meat-hook if memory serves. Never again. By the time we had managed to stop young Pike from screaming it was nigh-on morning. Stupid boy.

It wasnt just me! Godfrey wanted an armed escort just to nip into the bushes!

If your wood is damp then use a couple of drops of rifle oil. Be careful! You'll have to extinguish the fire at the first sign of enemy aircraft so don't build something so big it needs the county's fire service to put it out.

Walker,

I need a short piece about getting food in the wild, you know, hunting for meat using traps, poison, fashioning rudimentary spears and so on. I'd ask Jones (given his butchering background) but frankly he's just handed me what appears to be a novel about his time in the Sudan — I only asked him for a few notes about weaponry. As a man we often call on to provide supplies you seemed the obvious next choice. See what you can knock up would you?

Capt. George Mainwaring

Blimey, there's a world of difference between being a man who can lay his hands on a few choice items and being Tarzan... Traps, poison and rudimentary spears? Not exactly my style to be honest. Well... never let it be said I don't rise to a challenge [just ask the Womens' Institute Acrobatics Team].

Here's how I'd do it:

First track your prey [or local butcher] learning its habits [and the date of its meat delivery]. Then, when convinced that you know the best time to strike [when he can't move for cutlets rather than down to an ounce of brawn and a bit of scrag end] prepare your trap. Coax your prey towards the local watering hole [Dog and Duck] and engage its attention [get a few beers down his neck and tell him about your dirty cousin Doris who's staying with you for a few days]. While he's drinking slip a few drops of poison [large whisky] into him. Keep adding poison until effective [I suggest moving on to gin at this point 'cos it's cheaper and he won't notice]. To play for time, why not impress him with your rudimentary spear skills [game of darts]. Once the poison has worked, drag the beast [butcher] back to its lair [house] and skin it [get it into bed, make it a cup of Horlicks, night night squire where's your shop keys? Thank you very much, don't mind if I do...]. Then load up with meat so that you have plenty to keep you going [sell on].

'Ere Sarge, if I've knocked this out extra quick can I use up any extra space with another advert?

No

5. PREPARING CAMP FOOD
BY PRIVATE CHARLES GODFREY

Quite how the third reich would fear Godfrey is unknown, he looks so gentle here. Can we make this less tame?

Captain Mainwaring has very kindly asked me to offer some advice for the hungry soldier wishing to dine in the open. I was, of course, deeply privileged to be asked though I must confess that my sister, Dolly, has been of the greatest assistance. I'm no stranger to the kitchen but she really is an absolute marvel. Her scones are wonderfully moist and fruity, and she can perform miracles with shortbread. Not that I'm really one for petticoat tails, I prefer more savoury snacks. In fact I'm a terrible glutton for gentleman's relish!

Here then is our little twist on what I am assured is a camp food classic:

HEDGEHOG "EN CROUTE"   [Serves Four]

One large adult hedgehog

New potatoes	Green beans	Shallots
Mint	Butter	White wine
Tarragon	An egg	

A generous quantity of mud

I must say that I'm not terribly comfortable with the idea of eating hedgehogs [they've always seemed quite delightful little creatures to me] but Captain Mainwaring insists we remember there's a war on and that, frankly, it's the hedgehogs or us. The war makes barbarians of us all. However, if one must eat one of the poor fellows, let it at least be in a civilised manner.

First one rolls the hedgehog in mud, aiming to entirely encase its long spines. Ensuring that one's fire is smouldering at an even temperature [Dolly recommends around gas mark 4, though I am at a loss as to how one could gauge that accurately 'in the field'], the muddy parcel is then placed at the heart of the fire to roast for around an hour or so.

While that's cooking, take the time to top and tail some green beans. For the perfect 'al-dente' greens one should boil for around six minutes. The new potatoes will take rather longer of course, depending on their size.

When about fifteen minutes away from a perfectly roasted hedgehog, pan-fry a few shallots and prepare your *(1)* béarnaise sauce. Some might prefer hollandaise but I feel the musky flavour of hedgehog needs tarragon to lift it.

Remove your hedgehog carefully from the fire and peel away the hard mud shell. This should remove all those nasty prickles leaving you with a perfectly baked hedgehog. Serve with the vegetables and sauce. Might I be so bold as to suggest a relatively heavy wine to accompany? *(2)*

Oh, I have been asked to mention that if anyone has any trouble sourcing some of the — admittedly scarce — ingredients needed then they should contact: "Joe 'Caterer to Kings' Walker, Walmington-on-Sea 333" *(3)*

1. Perhaps it might be worth adding that you should take your own cow with you? Quite how one is supposed to cook this recipe on a weekly ration is beyond me...
2. Personally I would recommend something Spanish, a Rioja perhaps.
3. Ah...

6. DEFENDING YOUR CAMP
BY PRIVATE FRANK PIKE

This is Mums favourite photograph of me.

She took it.

It's about time I was asked to write some of the book!! After all I am the youngest in the platoon and my mother says I'm heroic. In fact the ladies call me Walmington's *(1)* Alan Ladd. I know Captain Mainwaring likes to dismiss my contributions, saying I'm stupid and childish and treat everything as if it's a game but that couldn't be further from the truth!! I'm just the devil-may-care, rugged, hero-type that's all and not even a bit childish so yah-boo sucks to you Captain Smelly Head.

Anyway, I've been asked to write about defending the *(2)* camp. Obviously because, whatever anybody else says, I am the biggest and strongest of the whole platoon!! *(3)*

```
1. One of the ladies, Frank, just one. Your mother.
2. You were asked to write about sentry duty actually
   but I see you've got somewhat carried away as usual
3. Given your age Frank, you certainly should be.
```

So, first of all: sentry duty!!

A) SENTRY DUTY

Sentry duty is of course, very very very boring. So the most important thing to remember is to think up some games to keep you going! Here's a couple to get you started

i. I SPY

You can't beat the old favourites!! Though it can be difficult to play in the dark of course [there's only so long you can hope to get away with "m for moon"]. One trick I've learned is to go for 'P for Pike!!' that always keeps them guessing. Though do remember to change it for your own name or you'll be cheating. Unless you're near a river, in which case you might not be.

ii. WHAT'S THE TIME MR. WOLF?

Be careful who you play this with. I once had a game with Lance Corporal Jones and he nearly shot me when I came up behind him. He'd forgotten we were playing a game and had assumed I was a "sneaky Nazi paratrooper wanting to slit him in the gizzards". Whenever I do play this though I tend to win. I think because I'm the only one who can actually run.

Oh! Another game you can play is "Keep an eye out for the Germans". I don't tend to bother with that one (1) though as it's boooorring.

I. Not if they turn up it isn't.

B) DEFENSIVE FORMATIONS

Another way to keep the camp safe is to actually build some defences. I'm always telling Captain Mainwaring that we should dig some trenches when we set up a camp on training. Not that we're really in any danger when we camp on Dimsett Field of course, I mean it's only ten minutes walk from home. In fact, if you shout as loud as you possibly can they can hear you in the town, though I wouldn't recommend it as it wakes up everybody in the camp and they don't half get cross.

A few trenches would still be good practice though, for if the Germans do invade. We could peer over the top like the Tommies do in the newsreels, waiting for the advancing hordes. I'd look brilliant peering over a trench I would, all moody and half-buried. We could always cover them over after so the cows don't fall in.

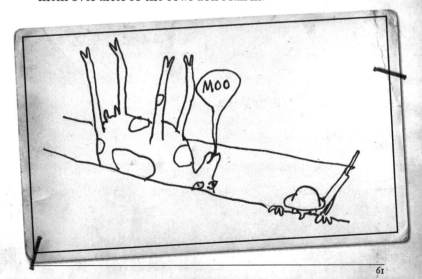

Either that or we could build one of those pill boxes [though why they call them that I don't know as you keep soldiers in them not pills]. In some ways I think they'd be good. It would be easier to stay warm while on sentry duty and you'd even have somewhere dry to keep your comics and your wireless. In other ways though I can't help but think they're a bad idea. After all, it's a bit obvious where you are isn't it? A German plane isn't going to be in much doubt as to where to aim: "I zink zey are hidink in ze big grey concrete zing, Hans," "Jah, Helmut, let uz drop a dirty great bomb on it."

Asking for trouble isn't it?

7. DEALING WITH THE WILDLIFE BY PRIVATE JAMES FRAZER

Can we go with a less-crazy looking photograph for Frazer?

Aye, trust a Scot to set you right on the dangers of sleeping abroad at night. When I was growing up on the wild and lonely Isle of Barra I saw some sights I can tell you, things that would make a bunch of English jessies like yourselves run screaming for your mother's apron.

You think it's bad in the woods at night here? Ach! You know nothing. When I was a child, bairns were often going missing, snatched up by starving gulls eager to feed their young. Death came from the skies in Barra so it did. Death with blood-stained beaks and a cry like all the devils in hell were screeching for ye!

And the moors... ah... don't even mention the moors, the nights were filled with the howling of rabid wolves as they hunted for meat. Oh, they'd eat anything, don't get me wrong, a wee rabbit perhaps or a stoat... well, who doesn't love a wee bit of stoat? But what they really loved, what they'd really got a taste for, was human flesh! Nothing filled a wolf's belly better than the meat of the young and unwary. Nothing it loved to sink it's dripping fangs into more than the soft, wobbling mass of a young maiden's fat thigh! *(1)*

Let's take a wee look at the worst of the indigenous wildlife in the English countryside shall we?

I. One senses that Frazer may have had to sit down for a moment here, perhaps take a few minutes to get over his own absurdly grotesque imagery and have a really good think about thighs.

A) FOXES

Oh, scared of a wee ginger doggie are ye? In Barra, toddlers used to ride these like ponies, just for fun you soft southern pansies. We'd wear a dead one around our necks to keep the chill off. A yapping wee scarf, that's what this is.

B) ADDERS

Adder? It's not even a proper snake. A bite from this would be no more than a bee sting to a Scotsman. It's just a fat worm, little girls on Barra used them as skipping ropes or to tie up their hair.

C) RATS

Don't give me that, it's nothing but a lardy vole. If it troubles ye then bite its head off and fry it up for supper like the hairy sausage it is. You're a wee girl, that's all ye are to come to me blubbering about rats.

D) MOSQUITOES

Mosquitoes! Wee buzzing things that are nay bother to any man who has enough sense to dab a wee drop of the embalming fluid behind his ears afore he goes out? On Barra the mosquitoes were so big they knocked you over when they landed on ye. My father used to take shots at them to practise his aim. What's next you hopeless sassenachs? Angry butterflies?

E) WASPS

Och... even worse! To a Scottish child anything this brightly coloured would be treated like sweets. They'd be popping them in their mouth and chewing them in no time. I bet they taste of your wishy-washy English flowers. Like Scottish flowers in other words but with all the flavour and beauty beaten out of them by taxation.

F) LEECHES

Leeches aren't a menace they're a form of medicine. Being afraid of leeches is like fretting over cough syrup.

8. CLEARING UP THE CAMP

Of course, once rested and ready to fight another day your platoon needs to pack up and march on. But wait just one moment, how best to cover one's tracks? The last thing a platoon on the move in enemy territory wants is to leave an obvious indication of their presence. Nefarious Nazi trackers could have you pinned down in moments purely by noting the angle of your abandoned cigarette butts.

But they'll not catch me and my men so easily!

During recent exercises I have encouraged the men to think of the abandoned campsite as a blank canvas upon which to paint the picture our purposes demand. We wish the casual observer to think we marched north towards the woods perhaps? Well then, we should march that way for a time before returning back along the same tracks and then leaving in the opposite direction, removing our boots and spreading out so as to leave as little trace as possible.

Or perhaps we wish to create the impression that we left the camp by the nearby river? So we break down the reeds accordingly, perhaps drop a few careless items such as empty rifle shells or a handkerchief. Our pursuers will be miles down stream, never realising that actually we simply crossed the river and marched away from the opposite bank!

Oh I know, this may seem unnecessarily complex *(1)* to some of you. Perhaps you even <u>consider it paranoid</u>. But you'll live to thank me with tricks like this in your arsenal *(2)* once the balloon goes up.

It can even be a valuable exercise in both fitness and morale for the men after a long night's sleep. Something to loosen up the muscles and digest the porridge! I let them take it in turns to come up with imaginative scenarios for us to enact, it makes them feel part of a team.

Except you never let me have a go do you?
Kidnapped by aliens?
Eaten by cannibals?
Attacked by dinosaurs?
You're never interested in the really GOOD ideas.

```
I.  A little.
2.  Just slightly.
```

PART 2 -
MAPS AND NAVIGATION
BY SERGEANT ARTHUR WILSON

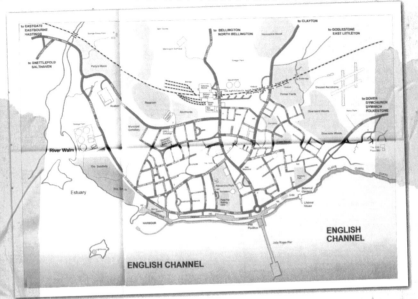

Aren't maps lovely? Like beautifully coloured pictures of the world as seen from above. As if you were floating on high like a pigeon or perhaps a starling. I have a lovely old map of the Lake District hanging in a frame, it really is most delightful to look at, one can stare at it for hours, imagining the landscape, the deep brown of the hills, the blue of the lakes. Lovely.

Of course, maps are also frightfully useful for getting about and are often used in the army as a method of getting from A to B without having to ask for directions. The army frowns on asking for directions. After all, if you were in enemy territory it's not awfully subtle and can often lead to awkward situations like imprisonment or getting horribly shot.

A) READING MAPS

The first trick of course is figuring out how to read a map. It's all very simple really and pretty much hinges on figuring out which way is "up". It's not always possible for the map makers to anticipate what direction you're facing and where you want to go so it's really a question of unfolding the thing and having a good old look. See if you can't spot something on the map [like a mountain or river or something] that you can also see in "real life". Then, when you've done that, decide whether you're to the right or left of this thing [or whether it's in front of you perhaps] and then pop your finger on the map at the point that seems to match. It's frightfully easy once you get used to it. What does help, of course, is recognising the symbols on the map as the landmarks they represent.

B) RECOGNISING LANDMARKS

Those clever fellows who draw maps have come up with a lot of clever symbols to help you recognise particularly important landmarks, you know, train stations, public houses, churches. They've even designed a couple of different symbols for a church so that you can tell if it has a steeple or a tower. Can't for the life of me

think why but I'm sure there's a very good reason. Maybe the person who designed it just really liked steeples.

Anyway, there's usually a helpful little key somewhere to tell you whether the dotted lines are footpaths or train tracks [often an important distinction] and the best thing is just to have a look at that and piece things together.

I've also come up with a few symbols of my own which I mark on the map once I've been somewhere so that if I go there again I'll know... well... what's what as it were. You may like to adopt these for your own platoon and update your maps accordingly:

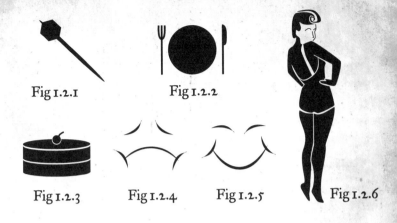

Fig 1.2.1

Fig 1.2.2

Fig 1.2.3

Fig 1.2.4

Fig 1.2.5

Fig 1.2.6

1. A pub with a dart-board, always worth knowing. It either means you can pass the time with a game or make a note to duck while you drink.

2. Decent restaurant, not one of those awful places filled with doilies and sliced bread.

3. Frightfully good cakes.

4. Difficult terrain for those, how shall I say it, "of a certain age". Be sure to check the gradient on the map [those wavy line affairs on the brown bits]. If they are too awfully close together then I generally add this symbol.

5. Simply gorgeous view.

6. Simply gorgeous view.

PART 3 - TRANSPORT
BY LANCE CORPORAL JACK JONES

(1) It is a very special honour indeed to be allowed to write a second section of this indispensical manual, This time Mr. Mainwaring would like me to talk about transport. He has asked me this of course as it is my lovely van that we use when we are out on special missions [and it IS a lovely van, whatever the lads sometimes say and whether or not it does occasionally smell of kidneys]. Here is a picture of my lovely van:

This gleaming beauty has long been a welcome sight in the Walmington-on-Sea area. When you heard my horn go "toot toot!"in the street outside you knew there was meaty pleasure on its way. And in these rationed times that's a treat indeed. Oh how people's faces light up when they see me out and about! You'd think I was Father Christmas with the way they behave.

Not that Father Christmas would have caught on the way he has if he'd made a habit of dumping offal in your stocking. No. I suspect it would have been a bit of a washout if he'd done that. Children want those little oranges at Christmas not liver. Liver's no fun at all in stockings. I think it's the wrong place to put it even though the housewife might normally welcome it with open arms though of course not when its in her stockings, they are for her legs, not liver. I imagine it would be quite uncomfortable if you put on stockings with liver in them. I can't agree with putting liver in stockings at all, the Walmington-on-Sea Gazette is much the best. Anyway, I can't worry about that sort of thing, I've got to write about my van.

People always smile when they see my van! Even more so now because they know that when it doesn't contain dead meat it contains the battle-ready action force that is the Walmington-on-Sea Home Guard platoon.

That is us.

To begin with, Mr. Mainwaring insisted on the van being conversant for gas, which I wasn't happy with I'll admit. I mean, what sort of vehicle runs on gas? The only ones I can think of are the camels we saw in the Sudan! They certainly seemed full of it with the way they went on. They sounded like the horn section of an orchestra being beaten up they

---

I. And possibly one from which the English language — not to mention the patience of the reader — will never recover.

did. Not that it's something you should talk about in polite company of course, if I am in polite company, it's difficult to tell when you don't know who's going to end up reading you isn't it? I mean, you might be the Queen for all I know. "God bless you ma'am," [just in case] "May I say you are looking radiant today?"

Perhaps we'd better forget I mentioned the camels. *(1)*

(2) What was I talking about? Oh yes, converting the van for gas. Well it didn't last, there were all sorts of problems, someone put a hole in it and we nearly lost control what with all the gas coming out [I sometimes think that Mr. Mainwaring should be more careful with the people he lets onto his platoon. Some of them are quite old and not as reliable as they might be. You wouldn't catch me being a liability like that when I start getting on, not on your nelly]. So anyway we scrapped that plan but it's still a formidable fighting machine what with the various portholes we've constructed in the side for to allow rifle access and a bit of the old bayonet! Yes sir, the cold steel on wheels so she is!

Not only is she a killer on both sides but she's raring to go on top too. A small hatch at the front of the roof

1. One will certainly try.
2. Gaseous camels but we'd better move on.

allows one of our many crack troops to expose himself and
point his weapon at passers-by. Or ask them for directions,
depending entirely upon the situation. In our case it's
usually directions, we don't get a lot of chance to shoot
the enemy you see, which is a great shame after all the
practice we've put in.

Of course I realise that not all platoons will be lucky
enough to have a nice van like mine. In fact many
platoons have no motor transport at all because petrol
is as rare as a nice steak and we all just have to make do.
So, in order to help those less fortunate than ourselves I
have designed a vehicle that can be used by everyone. Who
knows? It may just win us the war!

FROM THIS...

TO THIS...

THE LANCE CORPORAL JONES ARMOURED ATTACK BICYCLE

A) FRONT-FACING DEATH-SPIKE

First take an ordinary bicycle like the ones the platoon uses in the picture on the left. Then position the blade of an old carving knife like one I use in the shop just above the front wheel. Anything pointy or nasty should do it but beware! Because this is a lethal weapon which will kill Nazis when you are pedalling at top speed and bump into one but it will also embed itself in other things like bread vans too. I was half way to Hastings before I got free.

B) MULTI-DIRECTIONAL (FRONT AND BACK) HEADLAMPS

Tape two torches to the front and back so you can see where you're going and [in case of confusion] where you've been. Also attached is a device of my very own intention, the Jack Jones "Put That Light Out" switch. These are two toffee hammers held taut by elastic bands. At the first sign of an air raid you unhook the band at the front so that the hammer swoops down and smashes the torch, immediately plunging you into life-saving darkness. Can also be used to implement the bicycle's night-time "stealth" setting. The Jack Jones "Put That Light Out" switch currently has a single-use facilintity so only use it in emergencies. For regular darkness options simply adjust the on and off switch on the torches.

C) HAND-GRENADE DISPERSAL SCOOP

Conveniently placed within the rider's easy reach, this front-facing wicker scoop can be used to store grenades that may be flung gleefully at passing Nazis. It is also a good place for your packed lunch.

D) EMERGENCY ATTENTION-SEEKING KLAXON

For when you need to alert pedestrians that you are in a high-speed pursuit of a possible Nazi spy. Or just that you're about to ram them accidentally with your Front-Facing Death Spike.

E) FRONT AND REAR, REVOLVING DEATH FORKS

I drilled a small hole through the centre of the front and rear axles, I then inserted a thin pole with a cutlery fork on either end. These forks will now spin with the wheels and could probably be used to burst the tyres of enemy vehicles. I say "probably" because I've only been able to test it on a stationery tyre and the result was even more explosive than i expected. I panicked a bit, fell off and got the fork stuck in my unmentionables. So, on the plus side, i can certainly confirm the forks are good at attacking unmentionables. Should you spot any Nazi unmentionables drive into them at full speed.

Fig 2.3.1: Suggested simple version for those platoons that may still be struggling with allocation of weapons and forks and klaxons and such.

Sir,

I have here a photograph of the first version that I made in my shed. It wobbled a lot, and I fell off a few times. Sergeant Wilson thought I may have had a few too many sheeries, but I can assure you Captain Mainwaring, I would never do such

SECTION TEST

1. CLEARING CAMP

Come up with a scenario to mislead Nazi trackers as to your movements following a night's camp.

I would burn a pentacle shape into the grass, prop up the remains of a sacrificial goat and litter human bones around the place. When the Nazis came along they would be bound to think that, in an attempt to call on infernal powers to help us win the war, we had summoned the devil and he had eaten us right up. Like in that film with Boris Karloff. Actually, if Boris Karloff was available I'd pay him to be seen running off in the distance, that would convince them for sure.

2. HOW TO DEAL WITH DANGEROUS WILDLIFE
BY PRIVATE JAMES FRAZER

Right then you soft, wee fairy. How would you defend yourself against:

A wolf *I would hide up a tree until it went away.*

A nest of snakes *I would hide up a really tall tree until it went away.*

A tiger

Can tigers climb trees?

A flock of ravenous eagles

Erm...

— A —

Defend yourself? A sappy wee sassenach like you? You were doomed the minute the beasties clapped eyes on ye.

3. AN INITIATIVE TEST
BY LANCE CORPORAL JACK JONES

As you know there's no greater weapon in your armoury than your wits.

And your gun, that's probably just as useful.

But for the purposes of this exercise imagine you haven't got your gun and can only survive using your cunning.

You are being held prisoner by the Nazis who have invaded your camp. Using only your standard camping equipment [which doesn't include things like grenades, motorcycles and gatling guns... but maybe it should... if it did you certainly wouldn't be in this situation would you? That's a point, maybe I've solved my own question without even realising it! If in future you always carry grenades, motorcycles and gatling guns you could easily escape couldn't you? In fact they probably wouldn't have even captured you in the first place. Unless you were asleep at the time? Yes, that would do it, if all of you had been asleep then they could have snuck in and taken away all your equipment which would leave you back at square one. How would you escape now? It's beyond me...]

I would wait until it was morning and they were serving the porridge. Then I would use the porridge to build myself a false beard so that I could pass among the Nazis unnoticed. They would think I was just an old man, maybe gathering... whatever old people gather in fields in the morning... nuts or something... Once lulled into this false sense of security I would retrieve the grenades, motorcycles and gatling guns and win back the camp single-handed using the bravery and fighting skills for which I am famous.

1. May I be he first (of, I suspect, many) to correct you
   on that assumption?
2. Something of a mixed-up sentence this, perhaps
   better to take another sweep at it when less
   excited?

SECTION THREE
ACTION!

AND then, the moment arrives! Invasion! Oh I know that many people will see this as a bad thing but they haven't prepared for it like we have. We've been looking forward to stepping up to the crease for ages and it would be a hellish shame were the German team not to turn up.

In fact, I think I can go as far as to say <u>there's not a single member of my platoon</u> that won't relish the *(1)* moment Nazi jackboots take their first steps on British soil.

Now, everything that we have learned comes to the fore. These lessons are no longer just words in an extremely well-written and helpful manual but cold hard facts that are staring us in the face with their beady little Nazi eyes. No! Don't thank me just read on and fight well! *(2)*

PART I - KNOW YOUR ENEMY
BY CAPTAIN GEORGE MAINWARING

The first step to fighting your enemy of course is to identify him. *(1)*

The Nazi menace comes in all sorts of shapes and sizes but, whatever the uniform or disguise, there are some things they cannot hide.

FRONT VIEW

German Rifleman
Deutscher Schütze

Helmet, brim type, belt (Koppel), leather, buckle showing (Koppelschloss). Ammunition pouches, 3 each side, bayonet, short, sharp spade.

LEFT SIDE

An important note here: look at his eyes! Shifty, mean, set far too close together. These are the eyes of a typical Nazi.

Gas mask over right hip, canteen (Feldflasche) and rations bag (Brotbeutel). Long trousers tucked into half-length boots.

BACK VIEW

RIGHT SIDE

The main thing one would notice about a German rifleman from the back — and sadly it's not easily conveyed in a drawing — is his foul bull neck, red and puffy, bulging over his uniform collar.

It's a typical Nazi trait, no doubt linked to those foul sausages they love to eat.

I. Well, quite sir, all manner of disagreements could occur otherwise.

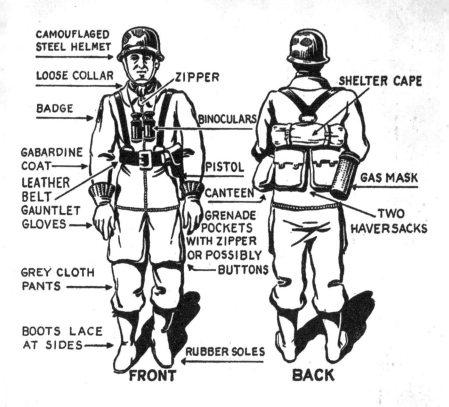

CAMOUFLAGED STEEL HELMET

LOOSE COLLAR

BADGE

ZIPPER

BINOCULARS

GABARDINE COAT

LEATHER BELT

GAUNTLET GLOVES

PISTOL

CANTEEN

GRENADE POCKETS WITH ZIPPER OR POSSIBLY BUTTONS

GREY CLOTH PANTS

BOOTS LACE AT SIDES

RUBBER SOLES

FRONT

SHELTER CAPE

GAS MASK

TWO HAVERSACKS

BACK

The main thing we notice here is the ears — no lobes —
very typical Nazi trait. I should make it clear that a simple
absence of lobes isn't quite enough evidence to convict a
man of being a Nazi. Though it is a solid start.

HERR WALKER HAS NO LOBES! HE
MUST REALLY BE JOSEF VALKER!

Leather covered steel helmet.

Parachute pack.

Web parachute harness.

Right hand on release grip of parachute.

Sub-calibre machine-gun attached to web belt.

Gas mask.

Iron rations

Pack.

Parachute harness

Other men carry grenades, folding cycles, entrenching tools, wireless gear, etc.

Most likely our first experience of the Nazi force will drop from the skies like this shabbily-dressed example. Typical of the Nazis to send someone out in what I can only describe as overgrown baby clothes. Built to inferior standards too I have no doubt. Likely to fall apart the minute it comes into contact with the bracing British air.

Not that we can necessarily assume these fiends will even be in uniform, according to recent intelligence they may come in disguise.

How is one to tell if the black and white shape falling
towards you is a sister of God or insidious Nazi? *(1)*
You may ask… luckily our platoon has hit upon a very
simple method: check the legs, Fritz may fool you with his
wimple but his ankles will never pass muster.

Ive never seen a Nuns legs, how will I know?

GENERAL POINTERS:

So, as we can see, there are some characteristics that always shine through. Whenever you are face to face with someone you don't know ask yourself these important questions:

1. Does this person have fine British ear lobes or is something amiss?
2. How big is their neck? Is it pink and puffy in appearance?
3. Do they sport aggressive and excessively colourful facial hair?
4. Is there an unusual smell to them? Perhaps the tell-tale whiff of stale garlic, cabbage and pig offal?
5. Are they wearing a conspicuous amount of leather? *(2)*

None of these may be conclusive taken in isolation but when considered all together be on your guard. As sure as eggs is eggs, if you find a stranger bearing all these characteristics you're likely to be nose to barrel with a Luger in a matter of moments and only a quick eye and a knowledge of the tell-tale signs will save the day.

1. One can't help but feel that the parachute is something of a clue, sir. Nuns are not really known as creatures of the sky.
2. This is all very well sir but, point for point, you could have been describing my dear Grandmother and I'm fairly sure she wasn't a german spy.

PART 2 - BATTLE STATIONS!
BY CAPTAIN GEORGE MAINWARING

*Wilson —
I like this one, but can we trim the edges for the printer?*

When Jerry marches into town we must be ready for him. He won't find the traditional, sleepy English streets or world-renowned tolerance of foreigners. His greeting will be short and brutal. But before the inevitable battle you must ensure that your town and the people in it are secure. Those civilians have been placed in your care by the powers that rule this wonderful country of ours, so live up to their faith in you and take control. Whether the townsfolk want you to or not.

It is vital that you quickly implement martial law. This will not be easy. While I have found that most people automatically respond to the firm hand of authority there will always be those that need forcefully bringing into line.

There will be complaints, accusations of un-democratic behaviour. They will call you names, like Little Napoleon the tin-pot dictator, just as an example, completely off the top of my head. I know, it seems ridiculous, but I have faced this sort of limp-wristed flannel a number of times during my service. I can only advise you to follow my example: calmly explain that their concerns and accusations are unfounded but that there is a clear need for increased security and protection. Then point to your stripes and explain that if people don't do what they're told you will be forced to have them shot. That should silence the naysayers.

1. ESSENTIAL RULES UNDER MARTIAL LAW

While details may vary according to your area, there are a handful of standard rules that must be adhered to in order to maintain discipline under martial law:

A) ALL LOOTERS WILL BE SHOT
The invasion forces will not be your only enemy. There will always be a portion of the populace that look to benefit from these circumstances. Last week during an exercise replicating invasion conditions in the town we had two young lads attempting to steal apples from the churchyard. Obviously, had it not been an exercise we would have been forced to shoot them.

B) PROTECT THE WATER SUPPLY

Nobody ever said the Nazis would play fair. They may well attempt to poison the drinking water. It is vitally important therefore that no water is drunk once the invasion has begun. The most rebellious quarters in this regard are often the catering establishments but I've found that a bayonet in the side of the tea urn usually cuts their selfish arguments short.

It is also important that <u>you conserve the water you</u> *(1)* have as the supply may be cut at any moment. I suggest no baths to be taken without a permit and all permits to be supervised by an officially recognised member of your platoon. Note: this does not — as was suggested by one of my more rebellious privates — mean that all baths should be supervised. Whether the bather gives permission or not there's simply no time for that sort of thing in a well-run army.

C) NO ALCOHOLIC BEVERAGES TO BE SOLD WITHOUT A PERMIT

Ah! This is the one that hits the rabble where they fear it the most! Speaking personally I've never been beholden to the attraction of alcohol. I will enjoy a glass of sherry at a party or a small beer when relaxing with my platoon but I have never seen the need for excessive imbibing. *(2)* To me, such things are an example of low moral-fibre. *(3)* There's simply no excuse for it. However, some simply *(4)* cannot help themselves and so it is up to us to be their moral guardians in this matter.

1. Surely if we can't drink it there's little point in conserving it?
2. Although there was that time when you were playing drinking games in the officer's mess and ended up so drunk you thought the sky was falling in, remember? I'll always smile when recalling your little red-face, spectacles askew, throwing punches into the air in an attempt to stave it off.
3. Or when you drank rather too much of the punch at the village fete (unaware of its alcoholic content I'm sure?) and attempted to wrestle an (and I quote) "obstreperous" oak tree to the ground.
4. Or when we shared a bottle of scotch after Mrs. Mainwaring had locked you out for the night and you ended up singing "Oh What a Lovely Pair of Coconuts" to the vicar s hatstand.

D) WE ALL STAND TOGETHER

It is vitally important that the townsfolk feel safe. They should know at every moment that the brave members of the Home Guard have their best interests at heart and are ready to protect them come what may. It is not a case of "us" versus "them". No. We are all one nation and stand proudly together.

Accordingly, all rumour-mongers, defeatists, nay-sayers... in fact anyone not obeying martial law should be shot. Nobody need fear for their lives while we're on the alert!

E) BREAK IT UP!

When I say that we all stand together I do of course mean it in a purely metaphorical way. There should be no gatherings larger than five persons allowed at any one time. Crowds breed dissent and the seeds of rebellion can grow quickly. Only the other day one of my privates overheard a group of air-wardens spreading malicious rumours about the efficacy of my troops. They were suggesting we were too old. That our senses were dulled by age and that we would be no use whatsoever when the invasion came. I was furious when he told me the details. Well, most of the details, Private Godfrey is somewhat deaf on his left side and he missed a good deal of what was being said.

2. SELECTING A SOUND H.Q.

A perfect base of operations is of paramount importance, a place that offers both the professional amenities you require and also the status and public respect of the residents. For many years we felt the Marigold Tea Rooms fitted the bill. Not only were there plenty of refreshments but the fixtures and fittings offered a number of ad hoc *(1)* weapons something that was of particular interest during the initial stages of our platoon when supplies and weaponry were thin on the ground.

In recent times, however, we have moved operations to the Harris Orphans Holiday Home Hut right on the front which offers a splendid view of the coast and the added advantage of two telescopes that enable us to keep a close eye on the horizon for enemy ships. Though the need to keep putting pennies in them is causing something of a strain on petty cash.

I. The rock cakes in particular were positively lethal.

3. GENERAL TACTICS

You will know your local area best and can think of tactics that specifically cater for your terrain. However, there are still a number of general points that apply countrywide:

A) SIGNPOSTS
The last thing we want to do should Jerry turn up is help him navigate his way around our green and pleasant land with the aid of signposts. Any platoon's first step then should be to remove signposts from their area.

A word of warning here: do plan a route before you begin. We split the platoon into several groups and a number of them were still lost the following morning.

Which certainly proved the plan to be effective.

We have experimented with a little twist on this by creating our own signposts and scattering them around the area. We have avoided local landmarks entirely, plumping for signs directing drivers to major cities such as London, Glasgow and Manchester. A number of these have also been placed at an upward-facing angle so as to confuse passing bombers.

B) SABOTAGE THE RAILWAY
We must stop the Nazis using our railway network against us, be it to transport troops or supplies. As soon as the signal for invasion has been given then hasten to your

closest line and destroy the rails.

Mind you, given how tardy most of the trains are around here I'm of a mind to encourage the Nazis to use them. On a recent business trip to Hastings I was fourteen minutes late, which would have been more than enough time to mount an ambush party had I been a carriage of Nazi troops.

C) MANHOLE COVERS

An excellent suggestion from GHQ is the removal of all manhole covers in the area, creating a potentially lethal series of simple booby traps.

Note: this is only really effective at night and one can expect a good deal of opposition to the idea from local residents. We tried implementing it as part of our nightly routine but were forced to abandon the plans after several fire wardens went missing.

Who on earth goes around photographing these things, Wilson?

4. FIELD ENGINEERING

The next step is to construct offensive and defensive positions. Don't just rely on natural cover, get the toolkit out and build some of your own.

A) STREET BARRICADES

Decide on the main access roads for your area and then get building. Barricades can be quickly and effectively built by whatever the keen platoon finds close to hand. Troops should be detailed to visit local dwellings and requisition suitable items. Chairs, kitchen sideboards, bookcases... all of these make excellent building material.

I can't recommend a platoon practice this enough in order to become thoroughly efficient in the art of barricade construction. Yes, the residents will complain -- nothing gets a civilian's back up more than stealing his easy chair in order to dodge bullets but they get used to it when you make it a weekly exercise.

Obviously you must leave some space within your barricade both to see through and shoot from. The important thing is to disguise these areas so they don't immediately draw enemy fire. The previous Home Guard manual suggested disguising these holes by covering the surface of the barricade in tin cans. Now, far be it from me to disagree but I can't help but think the idea is impractical in the time frame and potentially unhygienic. We at Walmington have come up with a cunning alternative.

Look at this:

Where do you think my platoon would place themselves in order to avoid the fire of the advancing enemy?

Could you guess? I doubt it!

We are in fact using a row of dustbins, one man per dustbin — for obvious reasons. A spyhole has been fashioned with a bayonet in the side of each dustbin to facilitate a good field of view of any advancing Nazis. Each owner has agreed to provide refreshment to the occupant of their dustbin in return for the platoon footing the bill for a new dustbin in case of mishap, being run over by a Panzer for example.

B) OBSTACLES

As well as defensive positions your platoon must look to constructing suitable obstructions for the invading forces.

As a seaside town one of our first steps was to weave liberal amounts of barbed wire on the beach to protect against attack from the water. It is now virtually impossible to move on the beach without incurring injury. As our patrols prove almost nightly.

For most platoons however, you will be thinking in terms of road obstruction. Here you will see we have required the townsfolk on this particular street to empty the contents of their front rooms.

My Lance Corporal, Jack Jones, has designed a lethal device — the Jack Jones Welcome Carpet — I am happy to share with you.

This is simply a section of carpet requisitioned for military use [the pattern is unimportant though we have gone for a civilised brown paisley axminster]. The carpet is then adorned with as many forks as your platoon can gather. It should be more than capable of handicapping most enemy vehicles, during our [admittedly unintentional] field test it proved more than a match for a motorcycle, delivery van and staff car.

Of course the Jack Jones Welcome Carpet will be no match for a tank. For this we have devised a different method entirely.

At various positions on the access roads to the town we have positioned milk urns filled with sticks of gelignite and scrap metal. These milk urns are, in effect, giant jam-tin "shrapnel" bombs. One of those rolled under the track of an advancing tank will do the job.

Do ensure you inform your local milkman that there are lethal urns in the area as a mix up could result in the loss of local supply.

PART 3 - COMBAT
BY CAPTAIN GEORGE MAINWARING

The town is organised and your base of operations is manned, now there is only one thing left to do: fight!

1. ARMED COMBAT

Now, I've heard many insubordinate Home Guard members bemoan the quality of their government-issued rifle. This is exactly the sort of rebellious twaddle I will not not stand for in my platoon. Yes, we have had to prioritise weaponry for those brave men who are fighting this war on the front but you'll go a long way to beat the rifles issued to us here on home territory. The Ross rifle is *(1)* at the very forefront of <u>British</u> munitions-production. It *(2)* is bang up to date and has been praised by fighting forces all over the world. Compact and light, especially designed for rapid fire and is the perfect defensive weapon for our stalwart troops here in England. *(3)* *(4)* *(5)* *(6)*

I tell you, when the Hun are staring down those Ross barrels they'll soon realise the game is up. *(7)*

It goes without saying that the key to armed combat is to keep a steady head and hand, pick your target and try and make each shot count. You should be prepared by now with sufficient rifle practice but — in case you have been unable to practise with live ammunition for any reason — I will point out that you must prepare yourself for the recoil of the weapon. It surprises all of us when we first experience it. In fact, my privates went flying when we first tried it.

```
1.  Canadian
2.  Twenty-six years old
3   Replaced by the (British) Lee-Enfield
    shortly after being issued to the
    Canadian army due to its extreme
    unreliability in adverse weather.
4.  Long and heavy
5.  But locks frequently in the damp
6.  Where it rains an awful lot.
7.  At least until we run out of the handful
    of shells we've been supplied with.
```

2. UNARMED COMBAT
BY LANCE CORPORAL JONES

Hello, it is I once more, writing in the book. He's a lovely man that Mr. Mainwaring, asking me to do three pieces, isn't he a lovely man? *(1)*

This time I am writing about the art of unarmed combat. I don't know why they call it an art though. I mean it's not like proper art is it? The painting of Haywains or Michael Angelo or what have you. That's proper art. That Leonard Da Vinci, he didn't punch the Mona Lisa did he? No, he was a gentleman. Probably. He painted her instead. Such a pity he forgot the eyebrows. "Art is never finished," he said, "only abandoned." I read that on a box of matches. I suppose that explains it, he abandoned it before doing her eyebrows.

Never mind, whether it's a proper art or not, that lovely man Mr. Mainwaring wants me to talk about unarmed combat so I shall.

Now, everyone who knows me knows that I am by no means a violent man. Just because I'm a butcher that speaks proudly of his time in the last war. About the many fuzzie-wuzzies I killed in the name of the King, about the things they do not like up them. A man who enjoys a bit of cut and thrust, a little bit of jab and parry, a slice of the cold steel...

I. Yes, Jonesy, lovely.

Where was I? Oh yes...

I'm not violent man.

But that doesn't mean that I don't know how to handle myself in a fight. I mean you have to don't you? Got to be able to stick up for yourself. I remember Kitchener once said to me: "It's not the size of the dog in the fight it's the size of the fight in the dog." Or maybe I read that on a box of matches too come to think of it, doesn't sound quite like the sort of thing he used to say. I mean, he liked dogs, I can't imagine he'd fight one. He'd win if he did though, oh yes... he would have had his gun you see. Never without it, typical soldier you see. A good soldier always knows where his gun is. Now, what was I getting at? Oh yes, unarmed combat.

Well the best thing of course is to not lose your gun.

PART 4 - COMMUNICATIONS
BY CAPTAIN GEORGE MAINWARING

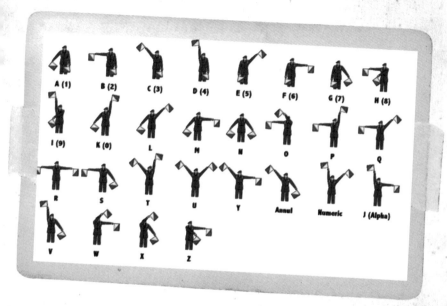

Throughout the process of battle there is nothing more vital than a clear line of communication. Imagine the catastrophe that could ensue without it. Just a few misheard words and you're shooting at your own men and blowing up the town hall.

I'm sure you don't need me to tell you that there can also be the odd problem with deafness amongst the stalwart, yet reasonably aged, ranks of the Home Guard. As such we have found one of the most reliable methods of keeping in touch at a distance is semaphore. Though some members of the platoon do have to ensure they have their spectacles with them in order to receive messages. And of course it's no use at night whatsoever.

During the hours of darkness we achieved some success with a lamp and heliograph but the response of the local Chief Fire Warden was so excessive we were forced to scrap it as a method of relaying messages. That and the near bombing of Private Godfrey when alerting the patrols that their tea was ready.

We did, briefly, experiment with a system of runners to relay messages between night patrols but found the recovery period for the runner in question was so long upon reaching their destination that any urgent messages were received far too late to be of use.

Unless we should be lucky enough to receive a radio set we are now almost entirely reliant on lined communication. This means we need plenty of loose change and a man on permanent duty in the HG office so that he can man the phone there and act as a central hub for communication.

It also means that we try and patrol as near to phone boxes as is practical.

PART 5 - PRISONERS OF WAR
BY SERGEANT ARTHUR WILSON

You know, sir, I'm not sure that this really strikes the right impression of someone prepared to interrogate a POW... Wilson.

Well now, once all that beastly shooting and punching is over and done with it's time to take a look at one's tally and see where one's got. Providing you haven't been utterly lacking common decency you may even be in a position whereby you have captured a few of the other side's men. The question of course is what should one do with them now one has got them?

A) LIVING CONDITIONS

First of all it's important not to treat then too badly. I know we're all terribly cross with them but that doesn't excuse our forgetting our manners. We need to make sure they have somewhere to sleep and a decent meal. By "decent" I'm not saying one should get carried away, steaks all around and "Would you like to see the cheeseboard?" but we're not barbarians are we? A few rounds of sandwiches will do until HQ's decided what's to be done with them.

B) INTERROGATION

Obviously we need to debrief the prisoners. They might know something frightfully useful to help the war effort. Now getting a chap to talk can be a somewhat tiresome business so here's a few pointers that I've found useful on the handful of occasions when our platoon have been in a position to interrogate prisoners.

i. THE SHAKE

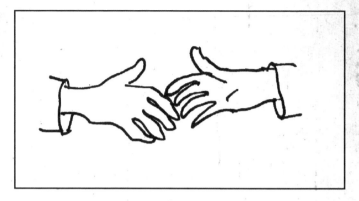

First take your dominant hand and extend it straight out in front of you.

Grasp the prisoner's hand firmly and shake up and down. Just because we're on opposite sides doesn't mean we need forget the basic gallantries.

ii. THE SMOKE

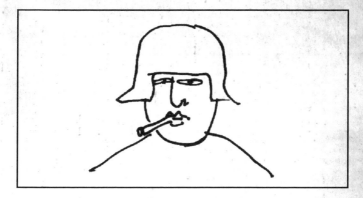

Then offer the fellow a smoke. Cigarettes are
wonderfully calming and if the pair of you smoke together
you may form a temporary bond

Light the cigarette for him, the act of a gentleman.
Do be careful to extinguish the match and dispose of it
carefully, we don't want to be like those savage Japanese in
their Prisoner of War camps

Tell him an amusing story, something to break the ice. I favour a devilishly funny tale originally told to me by Fruity Buckmaster from the Eastgate Platoon. The one about the three Nuns and a swiss cheese, you may know it? It's about these three Nuns who sit down to share a cheese only they haven't got any crackers. So the first nun goes to the Mother Superior and… well, maybe this isn't the place to go into that actually, now I think about it. Frightfully good though if you haven't heard it.

Anyway, once he's laughing why not ask him a few gently leading questions, slipping them in while his guard is down as it where. You know the sort of thing, 'Where are the rest of your platoon?', 'Why were you trying to blow up our church?', 'Do you have an accurate map reference for Hitler's bunker?" Whatever you fancy knowing really. Hopefully he'll be so busy chuckling about the cheese crumbs and the mice [or whatever your particular punchline is] that he'll spill all before he realises he's doing it.

IV. "SCOUT'S HONOUR?"

Of course the other problem one has to bear in mind is that the prisoner may not be telling the entire truth when he answers your questions. According to Captain Mainwaring an officer would never lie ["no matter what side they're on," he says, "class will always win out."] I'm not sure that's altogether true. I once had a great uncle who was a compulsive liar [in fact he was forever in trouble for claiming to be the tsar Nicholas II] and he was a member of the house of lords. But far be it from me to contradict my own commanding officer in these matters. All I will suggest is that you ask the fellow to swear and shake it on it, that way you are covering your back just in case he was making it all up.

I think you're being far too nice! They wouldn't do the same for you, they're all "Ve have vays of making you talk!" With torture and everything. I saw it in that documentary with Gary Cooper and Douglass Dumbrille

PART 6 - ESPIONAGE
BY CAPTAIN GEORGE MAINWARING

Of course it's not all direct combat. War is fought on many levels and a soldier must be prepared to indulge in the dirty art of espionage.

1) MISDIRECTION

Espionage starts with basic misdirection. For example: while queuing in the butcher's a few weeks ago, I announced my intention to discuss first-aid techniques during training that evening. This was not true. In fact I intended to show a fascinating slide show designed to help troops recognise foreign agents. I was simply sowing the seeds of confusion, allowing any potential enemy to think that the men of Walmington-on-Sea could be caught napping when it came to spotting an enemy in our midst.

Not that I believed there to be enemy agents present [though I have always been suspicious of Mrs. Ledwith's politics, any woman that eats that much corned beef must have sympathies in South America]. In fact I'm sure there wasn't. Having already seen the slideshow in question I would have recognised them instantly had they been there. Still, it's worth getting into the habit of this sort of thing. If you develop the practice of frequently offering false information it will keep everyone on their toes. (1)

I. "I think this section is very good, sir."

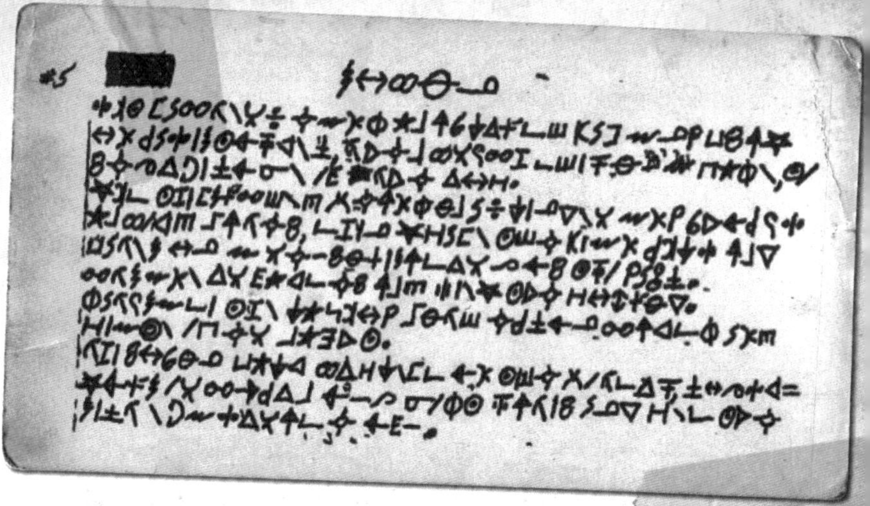

[handwritten coded symbols]

2. CODES

Alongside basic misdirection, codes can be used so that important information is disguised as meaningless waffle.

The Captain often talks in code!

Developing a code with your men is a vital first step in the secret war against the twitching ears of Hitler's spies. Once a code has been developed, a good deal of your open communication would be unintelligible to the enemy observer. Simply substituting key words for apparently meaningless alternatives allows all information both spoken and written to be safeguarded against interception.

When designing codes it is important to select words and phrases not likely to be uttered by accident during everyday matters. We had an incident here in Walmington-on-Sea where our local butcher [and Home

Guard Lance Corporal] set upon the mayor with his cleaver after being asked for half a pound of brisket. The phrasing of the mayor's order had led Jones to believe that the local dignitary was being used as a hideout for German U Boat captains. As ever with Lance Corporal Jones eagerness to serve got in the way of logic.

Our coding system works on a mixture of opposites [substituting right for left etc.] and word substitutions and is virtually impossible to crack without a full list of the code terms.

(1)

<u>Let me give you an example</u>, I might say to my men: "Jelly Pie for tea on Sunday, best tell Auntie Doris her leg needs polishing." By which they would understand that German planes were expected at four o'clock and that we should prepare patrol duties accordingly. ['jelly pie' sounds like 'Jerry fly', 'for tea' is '40', or four o'clock, I'm not putting the whole thing down in an easily intercepted book like this but <u>I'm sure you can see the form</u>] *(2)*

Slug soup at twelve for hungry horses!
Bottom-out the squirrels were hunting for whales!

It becomes a secret language that you share with your men, something that allows you to sit and discuss the most compromising details of forthcoming missions without fear of that information being leaked to the enemy.

3. CAMOUFLAGE AND DISGUISE

Not only must we disguise our words but also our appearance. Sometimes it may be necessary to evade or even infiltrate enemy forces and for that to happen successfully you need to be a master of disguise.

Let me show you an example:

'Who's that?' you may wonder. He looks a devilish fellow, swarthy and unreliable [although with an unquestionable glint of cunning intelligence in his eyes]. Well, you will no doubt be surprised to hear that it's me. Check my portrait at the start of the book and then compare. I know, it could be a different man.

1. Do you think that s wise sir?
2. NOBODY can see the form! It's a code so uncrackable only one man understands it, we just nod and hope things will eventually become clear.

The trick of course is not only to find the right clothes but also to "become" the character you wish to portray. When I was dressed as above I was disguised as a foreign spy, supposedly abroad on these shores to seed unrest. I spent a few moments staring into my shaving mirror, trying to smell that Baltic sea of "home", imagining the thoughts of such a crazed, political mind.

I also had a really good limp that looked excellent when I tried it out on the landing.

In fact I don't mind admitting that when my wife, Elizabeth, saw me returning up the garden path at the end of our exercise she locked the front door and refused to let me in. Even after almost half an hour of explaining who I was through the letter box she wouldn't budge! I had inhabited my character too well and slept in the shed by way of reward.

Here you can see another member of my platoon dressed in Nazi uniform.

Note the piggy little eyes, the weak jaw, the narrow, untrustworthy expression. All of these attributes made Private Frank Pike a perfect choice for this exercise.

Of course the danger here is that the impersonation will go too far, how long can a man stand to take on the lethal personality of a Nazi officer? How long before it starts to damage him mentally? How long before he really starts to think -- and act -- like the enemy. After all, only idiots and children have the mental elasticity to play dress-up for long without it affecting them.

This is another reason why Private Frank Pike was perfect for the exercise.

Oi! I vas in ze character! Like ze Lezlie Howards!

SECTION TEST

1. KNOWING YOUR ENEMY

How can you tell the above is a german spy?

Is it the ears?
I bet its the ears?

...There's just something in the eyes...

— A

1. CODES

Can you guess the meaning of these secret phrases?

i.   Tell mother the haddock's done, she can smack it
      till Christmas.

*Fish and chips for supper unless
I've been a naughty boy?*

ii.   Nobody likes a lightbulb fried on toast, it's the
      work of lame spaniel.

*Put that light out as
Hodges has got a new dog.*

iii. Bully beef for hair is all very well but how do you
      keep Skylarks in wheat?

*Can I borrow a comb? Mines covered in cow fat.
That cant be right...*

iv.   Jump onboard the fairy cake of springtime,
      there'll be no more nuts for us.

*Its probably something to do with parade,
Captain Mainwaring loves parades.*

You don't expect me to compromise our entire network by
decrypting these? What sort of fool do you take me for?

— A

1. CAN YOU RECOGNISE THESE PEOPLE?

Long John
Mainwaring

Farmer
Mainwaring

Herr
Mainwaring

Mrs.
Mainwaring

— A —
While you'll scarcely credit it, they are in fact all me,
Captain George Mainwaring.

AFTERWORD
BY CAPTAIN GEORGE MAINWARING

So there we have it, the cream of advice and training that myself and the platoon have developed over the years. You'll appreciate I'm sure that this is merely the tip of the iceberg. There are so many subjects we could have covered, so many more examples we could have given. But ultimately there comes a time when you must stop talking about it and simply get on with it. You know that as well as I do. You didn't sit at home when the call went out did you? You didn't talk about what you could offer. No, you stood up, took part and made it clear that you were happy to fight for what you believed in.

It doesn't matter what lies ahead. Maybe the Germans will come and we will lay down our lives. Maybe they won't. Maybe the war will end and all will return to normal. Maybe one day, many years to come, people will even look back on all this and laugh. They will laugh at the time when those silly old fools pretended to be soldiers. Well, no matter. Because we know that if our backs are set against the wall we won't be pretending. We'll be the last front for everything we value.

Well done. I'm proud of you. I'm proud of us all.

Captain G Mainwaring

First published in hardback in Great Britain in 2011
by Orion Books, an imprint of The Orion Publishing Group Ltd
Orion House, 5 Upper St Martin's Lane
London WC2H 9EA

An Hachette UK Company

10 9 8 7 6 5 4

Text © Jimmy Perry and David Croft 2011
Design and layout © The Orion Publishing Group 2011
Photographs on pages: 2; 6; 9; 12; 14; 24; 30; 36; 39; 40; 45; 48; 56; 59; 62; 67; 70; 72; 75; 84; 90; 92; 94; 97; 101; 102, 104, 107; 110; 119; 121; 124/5; 126 © BBC
Photo Library and Radio Times Picture Library

All rights reserved. No part of this publication may be reproduced, stored in
a retrieval system, or transmitted, in any form or by any means, electronic,
mechanical, photocopying, recording or otherwise, without the prior permission
of both the copyright owner and the above publisher.

Guy Adams has asserted his right to be identified as the author of this work in
accordance with the Copyright, Designs and Patents Act 1988.

A CIP catalogue record for this book is available from the British Library.

ISBN: 978 1 4091 41204

Written by Guy Adams with the approval of the creators of
Dads' Army, Jimmy Perry and David Croft.
Designed by Lee Thompson
Line illustrations by Michael Dover

Printed and bound in Spain

The Orion Publishing Group's policy is to use papers that are natural, renewable
and recyclable products and made from wood grown in sustainable forests.
The logging and manufacturing processes are expected to conform to the
environmental regulations of the country of origin.

"If there is another world, he lives in bliss
If there is none, he made the best of this."
because he went to:

JAMES FRASER

UNDERTAKER (& PHILATELIST)

GET YOUR LOVED ONES BOXED AND BURIED BY A REAL
PROFESSIONAL (AND FORMER HOBBYIST).

All pockets catered for: From luxury that looks too good to
bury to budget options for paupers or particularly unloved
family members.

DEATH - IT WAS BOUND TO HAPPEN IN THE END

HODGES THE *Idiot* GROCER

For all your fresh produce look no further than local hero Chief Air Warden William Hodges.

For all your rotten, old mouth compost
look no further than local simpleton
Chief Hot Air William Hodges.